Believe in Yourself

WHAT WE LEARNED FROM ARTHUR

Marc Brown

For my wonderful
family, all of you

ABOUT THIS BOOK

The illustrations for this book were done in watercolors, permanent ink, gouache, and colored pencils on cold-press Bristol paper. This book was edited by Andrea Spooner and Esther Cajahuaringa and designed by Véronique Lefèvre Sweet. The production was supervised by Virginia Lawther, and the production editor was Annie McDonnell. The text was set in Fairfield, and the display types are Fairfield SC, Fairfield Bold Caption, and Marc Brown's handwritten font.

Contents ◇

WELCOME TO THE WIT AND WISDOM OF ARTHUR!

A newscaster in Chicago once asked me to describe Arthur in just a few words. I told her that Arthur is an eight-year-old aardvark navigating the mud puddles of life. He doesn't always do it with great wisdom, but what eight-year-old does? What kids see in Arthur is someone real, like them, with no superpowers, who sometimes needs help from his family and friends. The characters in his world are never perfect. They make mistakes, get into trouble, fight with their friends. They show that you can learn from your mistakes and become a better person. Most of all, kids see that Arthur has a good heart.

Arthur has tackled some of life's smallest and greatest challenges, from head lice and bullying to fear and anxiety to coping with a loved one's cancer diagnosis. Characters with autism, dyslexia, and asthma didn't let these conditions define what they could accomplish. And they all celebrated when Arthur's teacher, Mr. Ratburn, married his special someone, Patrick. The books and the television episodes have tried to create a safe place where kids can see themselves and their families represented. Parents and teachers appreciate that the stories model empathy, forgiveness, honesty, and generosity—but kids love the humor, so we've never lost sight of having fun.

There's a magic that happens in that space between us and the pages of a book or on screen where imagination and real life can merge in a transformative way. My friend Fred Rogers called it sacred. He said that we can do a lot with that space, where *truth* is of paramount importance. And I like to think that one of the best things Arthur has done all these many years is tell children the truth. Children look to the media for truth. We all do.

Marc Brown

BELIEVE IN
EACH OTHER

ᘘᘛ ᘘᘛ ᘘᘛ ᘘᘛ ᘘᘛ

When the world seems a little lonely,
scary, or unknown, it helps to have
friends and family by your side. Arthur
and his friends have taught us how to
come together and believe in the very
best of each other and what we
each have to offer.

Sometimes the last person you expect will be there to support you! When Arthur rips his pants in school, it's Binky who is the first one to rush to help him, because he'd once experienced the same embarrassment.

Everyone in the cafeteria began to laugh.
Arthur couldn't move. But Binky grabbed two
trays to cover him.
"Quick!" he whispered. "Into the kitchen!"

—**Binky to Arthur**
From *Arthur's Underwear*

George has a hard time saying no to Buster, because he wants to be liked by all—but Arthur reminds him to be honest and speak up for himself. Being honest is an important step to building trust and fair relationships, and to believing in each other!

"You can't keep on saying yes to Buster every time he wants something. What if he wants your shoes next time?"

—Arthur to George

From "George Blows His Top" (Season 9)

Even the Brain knows that homework can be overwhelming—so he explains how to use an internet search. Give a friend some tips one day, and they'll return the favor in the future.

"Five pages! How will I ever write five pages? This must be what college is like, except we still have to be in bed by nine and can't drive."

—Buster to the Brain

From "Francine's Pilfered Paper" (Season 11)

*A*rthur and D.W. learn that to believe in each other, you have to get to know each other. When they end up in Mrs. Tibble's house on Halloween, they learn she's not the "witch" everyone thinks.

"I've waited all night for trick-or-treaters....
Years ago our doorbell never stopped ringing."

"Maybe it's broken like the windows," said D.W.

Mrs. Tibble nodded. "It is harder for me to keep
up with this big place these days."

"Maybe if we help you fix up your yard, the
place won't look so spooky," said Arthur.

—Arthur, D.W., and Mrs. Tibble

From *Arthur's Halloween*

Sometimes you have to really listen hard to what your friends are trying to tell you, even if you don't want to hear it—like when Francine struggles to sing and play the drums at the same time.

"What kind of friends are you anyway?
Why didn't you tell me I sounded so bad?"
"We all told you."

—Francine and Arthur

From the TV special "It's Only Rock 'n' Roll
(Starring the Backstreet Boys)"

There will always be a time in life when you think your parents are the opposite of who you are. But they're still a part of you and will always love you.

"They're not my parents....They just look like them. I don't know who they are."

—**Binky**

From "Kids Are from Earth,
Parents Are from Pluto" (Season 5)

When Buster confesses that he's not sure he wants to spend time at home after his parents' recent divorce, Arthur tries to help his friend by getting creative. Maybe a little *too* creative…!

"We'll dig a pit under my house and you'll live in it! They'll never find you!"

—**Arthur to Buster**

From "Arthur's Faraway Friend" (Season 2)

$\mathcal{F}$riends are there in the most difficult times. When Lakewood Elementary School is damaged in a fire and valuable possessions are lost, Sue Ellen is grateful to still have what matters most: her friends, who empathetically helped one another during this difficult time.

"This Friday it will be one month since April ninth. So much has happened since then. I never want to go through another fire. But I also never want to lose the feeling that each day is special, my friends are the best in the world, and that if we stick together, we can make it through just about anything."

—Sue Ellen
From "April 9th," Part 2
(Season 7)

When you struggle to find the right words, you can count on your friends— like when Francine is afraid of seeing someone she loves have cancer but doesn't know how to express it.

"I'm sorry I haven't come to see you. I just...I was afraid that..."

"You don't have to explain. It can be pretty frightening to see someone you care about when they're sick."

—**Francine and Mrs. MacGrady**
From "The Great MacGrady" (Season 13)

Even when a family member goes through a life-altering medical condition, we have to believe that they still know us and love us. We return that love by supporting them however we can.

"People change. The body changes and brains change too....But here's the thing: Your grandfather will always be your grandfather. He's still in there. And he still loves you very much."

—**Bubby**

From "Grandpa Dave's Memory Album"
(Season 15)

*A*rthur has to step out of his comfort zone when he is assigned the role of director in the school play, but no one wants to take on the most important role! His family and friends are there to support him when they see how far *he's* willing to step up!

"The turkey," Arthur began, "is a symbol, a symbol of...of..."

"Of togetherness and Thanksgiving!" said a chorus of voices behind him.

Arthur turned around and smiled.

"I guess Mom was right. The world *is* full of turkeys!"

—**Arthur**

From *Arthur's Thanksgiving*

*U*h-oh—Arthur and Muffy plan
their birthday parties on the same day!
Muffy declares that whoever doesn't
come to her party is *not* her friend, but
Arthur finds the value of compromise
in friendship.

"Surprise!" shouted everyone.

"Happy birthday, Muffy!" said Arthur....

"The rest of your party is on the way," said Francine.

"After all," said Arthur, "what's a birthday party without all your friends!"

—**Arthur and friends to Muffy**

From *Arthur's Birthday*

*A*rthur and D.W. prove that holidays are more about giving and helping when Arthur decides he's going to make Santa's favorite foods in one meal (which turns out to be a *really* smelly feast!). D.W. sniffs out trouble and swoops in to help save Christmas—and Arthur's dignity!

D.W. couldn't fall asleep.

"I have to do something," she thought. "Poor Arthur worked so hard. But if Santa gets one whiff of Arthur's present, he'll never set foot in the dining room—much less eat any of it."

—D.W.
From *Arthur's Christmas*

*T*aking responsibility often has the most surprising rewards. Arthur tries to prove he can take care of his own pet by looking after other people's pets! When grumpy Perky has pups, Arthur gets the best reward ever as a thank-you—
a puppy of his very own!

"You've done a wonderful job taking care of Perky, when she needed a friend the most."

—Mrs. Wood to Arthur

From *Arthur's Pet Business*

AND NOW...
A FEW WORDS FROM
D.W.

"Her name is D.W."
"That's it? Initials?
You didn't give the
kid a whole name?"

From "D.W. Goes to
Washington" (Season 2)

"I lose at everything. I even *lost* my glasses."
"I'll help you find them for five dollars."

From "Arthur the Loser" (Season 2)

"It's raining! We'll die out here!"

From "Arthur's Almost Boring Day"
(Season 1)

"Arthur has polka dots!"

From *Arthur's Chicken Pox*

"Now I know what true power feels like!"

From "D.W.'s Library Card"
(Season 4)

BELIEVE IN OPENING YOUR EYES, EARS, AND HEART

❧ ❧ ❧ ❧ ❧

*W*hen you open up your eyes,
ears, and heart to new perspectives,
new truths, and even new possibilities,
you discover how much the world has
to offer. Arthur and his friends
have shown us how!

When Arthur discovers in the second grade that a lot of people wear glasses, he realizes they're not such a bad thing, especially if they help you. Changing how you look can be hard, but your appearance will keep changing your whole life through!

"You wear glasses?" asked Arthur.

"Yes, for reading," said his teacher. He took them out. They looked just liked Arthur's.... Suddenly Arthur felt better.

—**Arthur and his second-grade teacher**

From *Arthur's Eyes*

*A*rthur sees what's *really* going on when Francine is being mean to him. This presents an opportunity for Arthur to be brave and stand up to Francine— but also to have empathy.

"I know you bully me because you feel insecure.
I hope you find a better way to express your inner
pain and anguish. Have a nice day!"

—Arthur to Francine

From "Arthur's Eyes" (Season 1)

*T*eachers seem to lead mysterious lives, but guess what? Teachers are people too! Buster finally gets a window into Mr. Ratburn as a person with a whole world outside of school.

"When [teachers] go home they sharpen pencils, eat kale, and dream up homework assignments. They don't even sleep. They just go into low-power mode and watch documentaries."

—**Buster**

"Mr. Ratburn and the Special Someone"
(Season 22)

When Buster does a report on his asthma condition, Binky's eyes are opened to what the inside of Buster's lungs are up against.

"I don't think I've ever been in anyone's lungs before."

—Binky

From "Buster's Breathless"
(Season 4)

Not everyone is the same in terms of how they communicate or how they experience personal interaction, George realizes when he meets Carl, a person with autism.

"He taught me to speak quietly, be clear, and not to take it personally if he ignores me."

—George

From "When Carl Met George"
(Season 13)

*I*n a special video, Mrs. MacGrady shows us how to acknowledge, respond to, and fight against racism: Talk about it, listen to one another's stories, and act!

"Racism is like a disease. If you don't treat it, it's just gonna get worse."

—Mrs. MacGrady
From a special PBS educational
video on racism

*B*inky takes responsibility for
doing something wrong and
apologizes…in his own special way.

"What I did was dumb and dangerous. It was also mean to all the Mighty Mountain kids who had been really nice to me. I'm very sorry, and I'll never pull the fire alarm when there isn't a fire again, the end."

—Binky to Mr. Haney, the principal

From "April 9th," Part 2 (Season 7)

On a tour of the White House, D.W. meets a nice man who happens to be the president. She is a shining example of confidence, truth, and never taking anything at face value.

"I'd have to know where he stands on the issues. I can't vote for someone just because he showed me a few pictures of horses."

—D.W.

From "D.W. Goes to Washington"
(Season 2)

*F*rancine is disappointed that Jenna wins the Athlete of the Year Award, but at the end of the day, it's much more fun to be happy when a friend wins something you may have wanted. It's called being a good sport!

"Mr. Haney! I am the captain of the softball team, the captain of the soccer team, the captain of the hockey team, the captain of the lacrosse team, and the only person who can sit on Binky's head. I should have won that award!"

—**Francine**

From "The Good Sport" (Season 6)

$\mathcal{B}$uster believes in everything—until his favorite show gets canceled for false reporting on the internet. Arthur and his friends remind Buster to examine what he finds on the internet with his eyes wide open for truth.

"You mean...just LIE? You really think someone would do that? Just go on the internet and tell LIES?"

—**Arthur**
From "Buster the Myth Maker"
(Season 9)

*A*rthur knows that it's better to use your conscience rather than rely on someone or something else to tell you what to do. When Prunella's cootie catcher seems to be foretelling the future, Arthur asks it an important question....

"Should we be obeying some old folded piece of paper? Or should we make our own decisions?"

—**Arthur**

From "Misfortune Teller" (Season 1)

$\mathcal{W}$hen we can hear what Baby Kate and Pal are thinking and saying, we view life from two completely different perspectives. It's a good exercise to imagine yourself in someone else's shoes!

"Grown-ups are slow, Pal. Look at how much trouble
I have to go through just to get my diapers changed."

—**Kate to Pal**

From "The Secret Life of Dogs and Babies"
(Season 6)

When Mr. Ratburn gets married to Patrick, we learn how important it is to support other people's happiness no matter who they love.

"We care for our teacher, and he deserves to be happy...[and] to be with someone who is nice, kind, fun...someone who likes him just the way he is."

—Arthur, Buster, and Muffy

From "Mr. Ratburn and the Special Someone"
(Season 22)

*T*reat others how you want to be treated! Francine hurts Fern by calling her a "quiet little mouse." And when Fern gets even, Francine is also hurt. If only they'd remember the Golden Rule!

"I always say, never serve anyone a stew that you wouldn't want to eat yourself."

—Mrs. MacGrady

From "Draw!" (Season 2)

AND NOW...A FEW MORE WORDS FROM D.W.

"This is one small step for me and one big leap for everyone else."

From "D.W. Aims High"
(Season 10)

"I don't like this place. It's full of people who make a lot of rules, and everyone's afraid of getting in trouble."

From "D.W. Goes to Washington"
(Season 2)

"It's your blankie....
I washed it."
"You killed it!"

From *D.W.'s Lost Blankie*

"I think baby dogs
should wear diapers."

From *Arthur's New Puppy*

"Saying D.W. is just a little
girl is like saying a tornado is
just a little wind."

From "Arthur's Big Hit"
(Season 4)

Organizational skills are important. Without order, you have a mess.
TUCKER

BELIEVE IN WORKING TOGETHER TO MAKE THINGS BETTER

*W*hen you choose to work together, you are showing kindness. Arthur and his friends believe in helping others, even when it's hard!

Taking action when you see
someone in need is part of being
a good neighbor and citizen.

Mrs. Tibble opened the door and turned on the porch light. She gave Arthur and D.W. a big hug. "See you Saturday to rake leaves," said Arthur.

—**Arthur to Mrs. Tibble**

From *Arthur's Halloween*

*A*s dynamic girl characters who raise their voices, Muffy and Francine become instruments for change! You too can be a leader and speak truth to power.

"In conclusion, over half the people on Earth are girls, so PLEASE create some decent girl characters."

—Muffy and Francine

From "The Agent of Change" (Season 14)

You can be a superhero every day in small ways! When D.W. imagines monsters under her bed, Arthur comforts her instead of teasing her. If you want to save the world, start with small acts of kindness.

"Sometimes being a brother is even better than being a superhero!"

—**Arthur**

From *Arthur the Brave*

How do Arthur and his friends work together when their favorite book series gets banned from the library? They recruit the Brain to save the day! By using research and facts, they protect their library from censorship.

"What we need to do is quantitatively demonstrate that we're not alone in our opinion."

—**Brain**

From "The Scare-Your-Pants-Off Club"
(Season 1)

When you have an important task to do, like preparing for a spell-a-thon, there's no one better to ask for help than those already by your side. Think of your community as a team to help you succeed in all your endeavors!

Arthur's family helped him study. Grandma asked Arthur his spelling words.

"How about your C-H-O-R-E-S?" Father asked.

"Have you made your B-E-D?" Mother added.

—**Arthur and his family**

From *Arthur's Teacher Trouble*

*H*ave you ever wondered how you can take care of our planet? When Mr. Ratburn asks his class to think of ways they can protect the environment, Arthur learns that even at home, each of us can make a global difference.

"I found things I can do to save energy in almost every room."

—Arthur

From *Arthur Turns Green*

*C*amp isn't so bad after all when Arthur ends up working together with his friends to win the scavenger hunt. He's carrying the final object— right in his hands! Hooray for friends working together!

"A flashlight!"
"We won!"
"Three cheers for Arthur!"

—Arthur and friends

From *Arthur Goes to Camp*

Believe in Yourself

∽♡∽ ∽♡∽ ∽♡∽ ∽♡∽ ∽♡∽

*A*t the end of the day, always
remember to believe in yourself.
Confidence is key, but so is embracing
who you are! Arthur and his friends
celebrate who they are every single
day, and so can YOU!

$\mathcal{H}$ave you heard the saying "practice makes perfect"? D.W. proves that when she sees that sometimes you have to keep trying, until eventually you get the hang of something new.

"I don't care if it takes till I'm twenty-one and I'm one giant scab. I'm gonna learn to do this."

—D.W.

From "D.W. Rides Again" (Season 1)

$\mathcal{B}$uster may be just a kid, but he's
lucky to discover that the greatest job you
can have is doing work that you love.

"He gave me seventy-three cents, a sticker of a cool car, and a button for my joke. I got paid for writing a joke! I'm a professional!"

—**Buster**

From "Buster's Growing Grudge"
(Season 3)

Have you ever had to face a big moment? When Arthur is asked to write a speech, he needs help, and D.W. rises to the occasion. She has confidence to spare!

"I'll make the speech for you. I have a
lot of ideas about how to run the country."

—D.W. to Arthur

From *Arthur Meets the President*

*E*veryone may have an opinion about what you write, share, or say to others—but when you write, think about being true to yourself.

"Don't worry about what you think people want to hear. Just tell your story the way it means the most to you."

—Mr. Ratburn

From "Arthur Writes a Story"
(Season 1)

*I*f you feel good about yourself, you'll notice that you smile a little more and are happier around others—and they'll be happier around you! It's okay to feel all your emotions, but if you're feeling extra grouchy, tell someone who will listen and support you.

"Nobody likes a grouch, so smile a little!"

—D.W.

From *D.W.'s Guide to Perfect Manners*

*H*ave you ever had to overcome an obstacle? George discovers he has dyslexia and is afraid of being honest with his friends—but they support him no matter what.

"Wally, I need your advice. Kids are finding out how much trouble I have reading and writing and stuff."

—George to his puppet, Wally

From "The Boy with His Head
in the Clouds" (Season 6)

$\mathcal{D}.\mathcal{W}.$ "wrote the book" on believing in yourself! With this kind of conviction, you can do anything. Now get out there and do it!

"That sign can't stop me, because I can't read!"

—D.W.

From "D.W.'s Name Game" (Season 2)

BELIEVE IN
A WONDERFUL
KIND OF
DAY. HEY!

*A*lways leave room for fun,
imagination, and play! You can count
on Arthur and his friends to discover
and share the joy, laughter, and silliness
in all the moments life has to offer.

*F*un comes in all places, shapes,
and sizes—and libraries unlock an
unlimited number of worlds, both
real and imagined.

"Having fun isn't hard when you've got a library card!"

—**Arthur and friends**

From "Arthur's Almost Live Not Real Music Festival" (Season 3)

With rain every day, Arthur thinks his vacation is doomed. But he also shows us that with imagination and problem-solving, you can fill your day with fun.

"I never realized there are so
many fun things to do in the rain."

—Dad

From *Arthur's Family Vacation*

*W*hen the internet service goes out, the gang panics—but then discovers that the world continues on, and there's still fun to be had, despite their initial disbelief.

"Guys, I think the internet is...gone."
"That can't happen, can it?"

—Arthur and LaDonna

From "The Longest Eleven Minutes" (Season 22)

*H*ave you ever wished you were older? In true D.W. form, after she watches a TV show about fancy weddings, she immediately decides she can't wait. Hint: Being a kid is more fun. Enjoy it!

"My dad said I could have a wedding when I'm older. That was an hour ago. And now I'm older....You get to be my bridesmaid!"

—D.W. to Emily

From "D.W. Unties the Knot" (Season 14)

*T*ime goes slowly when you're away
from those you love. Kate and Pal are
best friends, but we learn just how much
Pal relies on Kate when they have to
be separated.

"Goodbye, dearest Kate. I know it shall
only be for an hour, but it will feel like
seven hours to me!"

—Pal to Kate

From "The Secret Life of Dogs and Babies"
(Season 6)

*D*on't let self-consciousness get in the way of fun! Jenna's afraid to go to Muffy's slumber party because she wets the bed, but she learns that it's no big deal. We all have embarrassing things happen sometimes!

"And then someone said they remembered me from when I was in diapers."

"Everybody wore diapers. It's what we did. Why do adults bring it up?"

—George and Buster

From "Jenna's Bedtime Blues" (Season 7)

When Muffy, Buster, and Arthur
attend a cooking class with a famous
chef, he dishes out some classic wisdom
about so many situations in life!

"I was trying to not make a mess."
"Cooking is messy! Life is messy! You must
enjoy the mess!"

—Muffy and Francois Puffeau

From "Buster's Carpool Catastrophe" (Season 15)

BELIEVING IN ARTHUR
How Arthur Came to Be

MAKING BOOKS

I was literally rescued by Arthur.

It was 1975, and the college where I was teaching closed. I was suddenly unemployed and I was worried—what was I going to do now? And then, a bedtime story for my son changed my life: "This is Arthur. He is worried about his nose." Arthur was worried about something too. And there was the answer, right in front of me: I would tell stories, just like my grandmother and great-grandmother had done for me and my sisters. We loved Grandma Thora's spooky stories and would squeal with joy and horror when she took out her false teeth.

For each and every one of us, our childhood plays an important part of who we are and what we become. Most people grow out of their childhood; I grew back into mine when I started making books. My memories became the beginning of Arthur's imagined world. I could vividly remember the joys, heartbreaks, messiness, and dignity of being a third grader. Right there in Miss Kingston's third-grade classroom, that's where it all began. In elementary school, I got into some trouble for daydreaming and drawing during class. Now it's my job!

Because all the characters in Arthur's world were inspired by my classmates, family, and teachers, kids feel they're authentic and sometimes completely real. I once got a letter from a young reader asking for Francine's phone number! (Speaking of phone numbers: After I put our real home phone number in the art of *Arthur's Thanksgiving,* every November the calls would begin: "Is Arthur there?" My wife, Laurie, had the best response: "No, he's at the

Marc Brown in third grade

library." We have since moved, so don't get any ideas!) Kids want to believe that aardvarks go to the library and school and have issues just like they do. They believe in the worlds that writers and artists bring to life, and because of that, books can be magical. It's the most important thing I've learned as an author and illustrator.

Creating the magic isn't easy, though. There are no born writers. I have many erasers! I make lots of mistakes. I've often done as many as thirty drafts of each story before I show it to the publisher. Then my editor saves the day with wonderful suggestions. My first book, *Arthur's Nose,* was published in 1976, after six long months of revisions. And in the process, I learned that a picture book is like a delicate scale, with words on one side and pictures on the other. You use words to do only what your pictures can't do.

My stories usually begin with an incident that happened to me as a child or to my kids while growing up. Sometimes kids tell me what they want Arthur and his friends to do next. *Arthur's Underwear* grew out of a request I heard so many times that I had to write the book. (Why is the word *underwear* so hilarious?) Whatever story I'm writing, I always try to make readers laugh. I think kids learn best through humor. I get excited about taking kids into a new space that will change the mood. If kids read a book about an aardvark wanting a pet, they're not looking for plausibility or logic. When they open a book about Arthur, they're expecting fun.

In 2002, I celebrated with Carol Greenwald at the Emmys, where Arthur *won Best Animated Children's Program.*

MAKING TV SHOWS

One sunny April day in 1993, as I was finishing the art for the twenty-third book in the series, *Arthur's New Puppy*, the phone rang. It was Carol Greenwald, a television producer at WGBH in Boston. She and her kids had attended a talk I gave at the Winchester Public Library, and now she wanted to use Arthur for an animated TV show to inspire kids to read. What a great idea! I soon learned that Carol had lots of great ideas, and she would guide Arthur to become the longest-running animated children's show in history.

After fifteen years of having Arthur all to myself, sharing him with others was probably the most difficult thing I had to do. Suddenly I was part of a team...and they were asking so many questions! Can you draw a floor plan of Arthur's house? How does Arthur walk? What's Francine's family like? Where does Buster live? Can you make a map of Ellwood City for the animators? How can we be most inclusive, showing characters from different cultural backgrounds, socioeconomic levels, and family situations, as well as with various disabilities and religious identities? I had entered a whole new world and feared I might not be ready for it.

But right away I was struck by how similar making books and TV shows actually is. You still write your story, cast and costume your characters, and design the sets. But with animation, we had the luxury of sound and movement. I could shout "Action!" instead of being forced to pick just one moment to freeze-frame in a single scene.

With my nephews Leo and Julian, Emmy Award thieves caught in my studio.

Like with picture books, the script is the foundation of each episode and it must be strong. We're not looking to fill our eleven-minute episodes with frenetic nonsense or violence. Kids deserve better. This is serious work. Each member of the team comes to the annual writers' meeting with a list of story ideas. Pitches can be as funny as "Where do all our socks go?" or as short as two words: "desk wars." One of the writers will find an affinity for a specific idea and a gem of a story will emerge.

Finding writers who understood kids was critical. I remember interviewing our first head writer, Kenny Scarborough, and seeing his face light up when I asked him about his childhood. When he told me that his mom let him and his brother pick out the new wallpaper for the dining room—a Wild West cowboy theme—and that they lobbied to replace the dining table with a pool table, he got the job. Connecting with a genuine childlike mindset is what makes a great *Arthur* script.

I learned quickly how a director can help shape a story by knowing the possibilities and limitations of animation. After twenty-five years, Greg Bailey has directed every single *Arthur* episode with a command of the craft and an encyclopedic knowledge of the content from hundreds of episodes. (We'd better remember what our characters did in each story, because kids sure do!) We sprinkle humor for adults in every episode too, hoping to engage parents and caregivers to watch along with kids. When you share a book or a TV show with a child, you have a powerful opportunity to extend that story in personal ways to share your own values and ideas. I like to think we begin conversations for families.

The day I met Fred in his Pittsburgh office, I made this drawing of him.

MAKING FRIENDS

One of the most rewarding aspects of working on the show was getting to know the talent behind the scenes. Fred Rogers was one of our first guest stars on *Arthur*, and he became a great friend. The day I probably treasure the most with Fred was when he came to my studio to film a show about demystifying animation for kids. While the crew was setting up, we had time to talk. Fred said, "Tell me about your grandma Thora." It was as if he had reached right into my soul. Tearing up, I told him how she would save two or three dollars a week for my college education, and how once she opened her bottom dresser drawer and there were all the drawings I had given her. Fred said she sounded a lot like his grandfather, a special person in his own childhood. And then he said something I will never forget: "Every child needs just one person to believe in them to make it."

I often think about this when I meet teachers. So many of them become that "one person" who changes lives. Good teachers care deeply about their students and make profound differences in the lives of many children. Teachers are my heroes. Every day they are quietly helping to shape the next generation of citizens and leaders.

I certainly wouldn't be doing what I'm now doing if it wasn't for Nancy Bryan, my high school art teacher. One day she told me to get my portfolio and drove me to the Cleveland Institute of Art for an interview. I left that day with an invitation to return in the fall on a full scholarship.

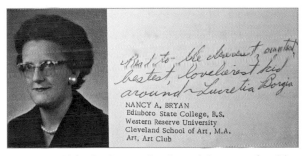

NANCY A. BRYAN
Edinboro State College, B.S.
Western Reserve University
Cleveland School of Art, M.A.
Art, Art Club

In 1964, my high school art teacher changed the course of my life.

MAKING IT

Arthur has been our friend now for over forty-five years, and his show has been enjoyed for over twenty-five years. For me, the best part of the Arthur experience has been getting to speak to kids across the country. The thing that always impressed me most about them was their honesty. At the end of a school visit in Dallas, Texas, I asked a class if they had any questions, and an eager second grader quickly raised his hand. "If you're a famous author, how come you aren't dead?" he asked. Next question!

I was asked to speak at a university to students who would soon graduate. As I struggled with writing my talk, I asked my youngest son for some suggestions. "They are *freaking out*, Dad! Just give them some advice about what to do."

In 1997, Arthur debuted at the Macy's Thanksgiving Day Parade in New York City. Arthur was one of seven giant balloons to make it all the way to 34th Street on a very windy day.

Arthur and his friends almost wrote the speech for me.

WHAT I LEARNED FROM ARTHUR:

1. **Expect detours.** D.W. would tell you that "you're in BIG TROUBLE. The worst is yet to come!" Arthur would add that detours can offer adventures, discoveries, and opportunities.

2. **Be assertive.** Go after what you want. Each of us is capable of making powerful commitments, but first we need an extraordinary goal.

3. **Be nice.** Remember to say "please" and "thank you"—and a sense of humor can be helpful too.

4. **Accept help and offer it too.** We are all in this together.

5. **Know your business; know who you are.** People are drawn to those who are strong and know who they are. Be that person.

6. **Always tell the truth.** You are only as good as your character and conscience.

7. **Life is a process.** Maybe Fred Rogers said it best: "Discovering the truth about ourselves is a lifetime's work, but it's worth the effort."

8. **No matter how hard we plan, destiny takes over.** Be open to change. It's not all about you.

9. **True success is doing what you love to do.** Make a commitment to go after your best. Love what you do, and if you don't love what you are doing, keep looking. Now, go out there and stay strong and keep dreaming.

Arthur will always be eight years old. The rest of us have grown up over the years, and I like to think that Arthur has helped us do that. Little did I know, way back in 1976 when I wrote that last line in *Arthur's Nose*—"There's a lot more to Arthur than his nose"—just how true that would really be.

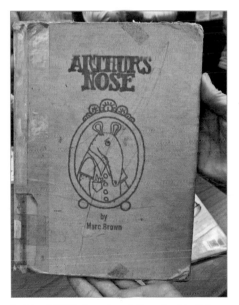

In March 2020, I went to visit a school in Erie, Pennsylvania, where I grew up, and the librarian showed me their well-read copy of Arthur's Nose.

Acknowledgments

"Only the rarest kind of best can
be good enough for the young."
—Walter de la Mare

*H*ow's that for a high bar? This book would not have come to be without a superb Arthur team who helped shape the many Arthur books and television programs with knowledge, love, and care. Together we have always aimed for that high bar, looking at the world to find what is meaningful to children and why. And where would I be without the many children who welcomed me into their imaginations and decided I was funny? You allowed me to do what I loved most as a child: daydream and draw. Thank you.

My gratitude to the Cleveland Institute of Art, where the faculty always encouraged me to experiment—and where five years of study taught me, among many other things, that an element of mystery is always helpful.

I am fortunate to work with three distinguished publishers: Little, Brown and Company, who first took a chance with me (and this book is witness to their enduring confidence and support); Random House/ Knopf, who helped me connect to the youngest Arthur viewers; and my newest friends at Scholastic.

To Emilie McLeaod, my first editor, who saw something in me that I couldn't. To the extraordinary editors and art directors who have shared their precious time, teaching me so much over the past forty-some years: Janet Schulman, Ole Risom, Ted Geisel, Melanie Kroupa, Maria Modugno, Cathy Goldsmith, Ann Durrell, Riki Levinson, Phyllis Fogelman, Isabel Warren-Lynch, Nancy Hinkel, Liza Baker, Patti Ann Harris, and of course the team of Andrea Spooner, Véronique Lefèvre Sweet, and Esther Cajahuaringa, who helped me tell this story.

Special thanks are also due to my television family: Carol Greenwald, who thought it should happen, and Alice Cahn and Linda Simensky at PBS, who made it happen; my hero, Fred Rogers; Tina Cassidy, Leslie Taylor, Casandra Schaffausen, Diane Dillaire, Toper Taylor, Ron Weinberg, Micheline Charest, Bridgid Sullivan, David Bernstein, Jeff Garmel, Margot Nassau, Deb Frank, Geoff Adams, Pierre Valette, Kathy Waugh, Jacqui Deegan, Greg Bailey, head writers Peter Hirsch, Ken Scarborough, Joe Fallon, and the many other brilliant writers; my son and producer, Tolon Brown; Michael Yarmush and Michael Caloz, the first voices of Arthur and D.W., along with director Deb Toffan and the best cast of voice actors I could ever hope for; Gerry Capelle and all the terrific storyboard artists; Ziggy Marley and our many guest stars who helped make some of our most important stories come to life.

A few of the many who made this journey sweeter: my Moscow amigos R. L. Stine and Peter Lerangis, and Laura Bush, who took us there; Steve Krensky, Paula Danziger, Marilyn Hafner, Patrick Bell, Jim Marshall, Judy Sue Goodwin-Sturges, George and Barbara Bush, Bob Freedman,

Richard O'Connor, Michael Barron, and Rich Michelson; Jackie Hartnett, Pamela Dixon, and the 35 North Street team; Steven and Helen Kellogg; Ed Emberley, who explained the "escalation clause"; Mike and Ann Shilhan, Jill and Chuck Crovitz, Dave and Beldan Radcliffe, the Druckmans, all our friends at the American Folk Art Museum, Mary Etta and John Bitter, Suzan Bruner, and Tara Maiello; the Hyde School in Bath, Maine; my sisters, Bonnie, Coll, and Kim; my superior kids and grandkids, Tolon, Tucker, Eli, Christina, Skye, and Bella; and the many special people I don't have space to mention here.

The biggest, bestest thanks goes to my partner, co-collaborator, and wife, Laurie Krasny Brown, from whom I learned the importance of order and that even the interior of a refrigerator can be a work of art. I am grateful to her for more than I can say. And I have learned that love is the best rudder a guy could ever have.

Like a trapeze artist, or a parent, an author needs courage, trust, and most important, knowing when to let go. It's a concept I struggle with. It's my hope that this last Arthur book celebrates the gifts from each of you that helped shape this glorious adventure.

Now, onward I go, with new projects unfolding. Authors and artists never retire. Isn't life wonderful?

—Marc Brown